Seasick

Written by Roderick Hunt
Illustrated by Nick Schon,
based on the original characters
created by Roderick Hunt and Alex Brychta

Say the sound and read the words

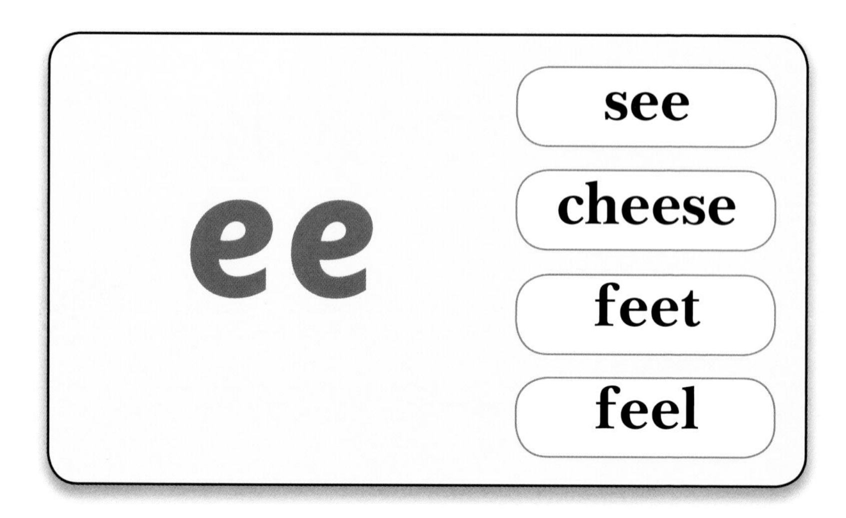

ea

sea

beach

seat

cream

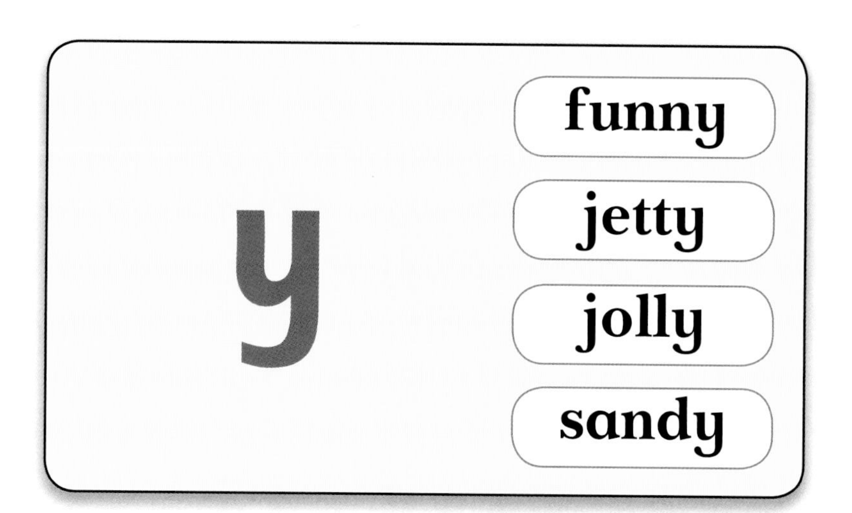
y
funny
jetty
jolly
sandy

Gran had a hut, by the sea.

"It's my beach hut," said Gran.

“I call it Sandy Feet,” she said.

Gran had six seats in the hut.

They had a picnic.

“Cheese rolls,” said Gran. “Then jelly and cream.”

"What a picnic," said Biff.
"It's a feast."

Gran had a boat at the jetty.

"I call it Jolly Jean," she said.

It was fun in Jolly Jean.

“I can see a seal,” said Chip.

But then the sea was choppy.
The boat went up and down.

“My tummy feels funny,”
said Wilma.

“Sorry,” said Gran. “We had too much jelly and cream.”

They went back to the beach hut.

"Beans on toast?" said Gran.

Talk about the story

Why didn't the children want beans on toast?
What part of the day do you think the children enjoyed the most? Why?
What would you like to eat for a feast?

Word jumble

Make the *ee*, *ea* and *y* words from the story.

ch b ea

ll j y e

ch ea

ch pp o y

l ee f

e y j tt

ee s

ea s t

ee, ea or y?

The sound 'ee' can be spelled *ee, ea* and *y*. Match the right 'ee' spelling to the pictures and complete the word.

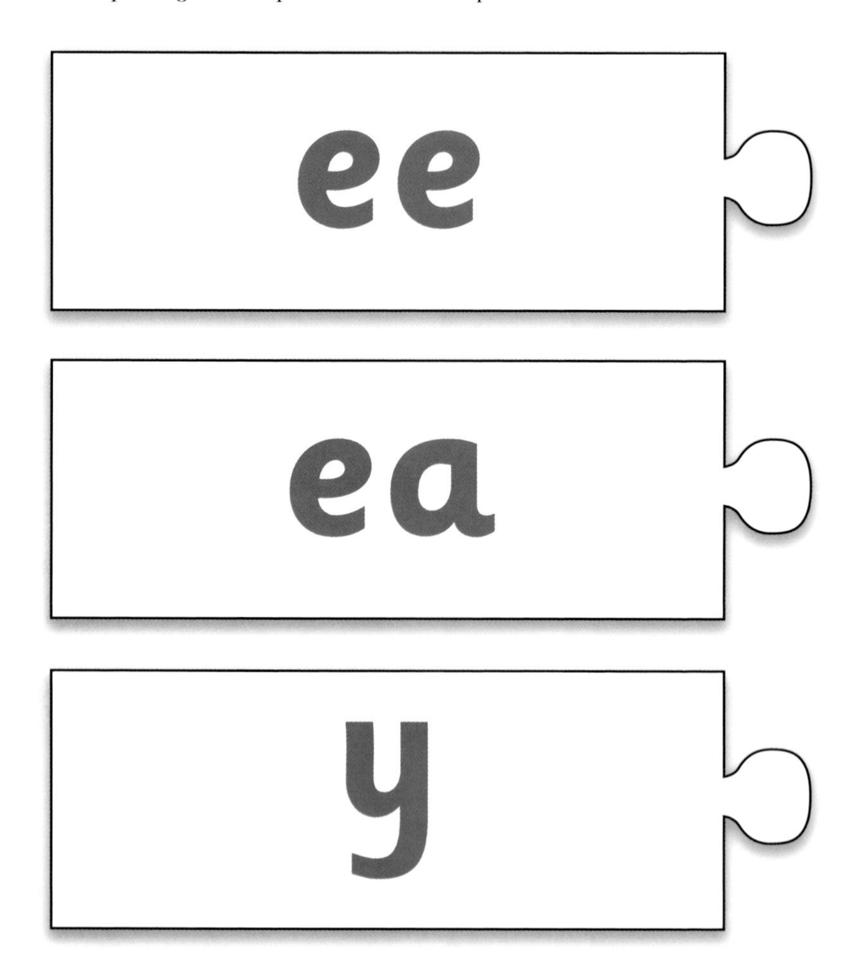

s__
Joll_ J__n
Yummi
Baked
Beans
b__ns
ch__se
s__l
f__t

Find the *ea* words

Read the words. Point to the ones you can find in the picture.

beach   beans   feast   Jolly Jean

sea   seal   seasick   seat